HAPPY BIRTHDAY, MOON

A MOONBEAR Book

· FRANK ASCH ·

ALADDIN

NEW YORK   LONDON   TORONTO   SYDNEY   NEW DELHI

ALADDIN

An imprint of Simon & Schuster Children's Publishing Division

1230 Avenue of the Americas, New York, NY 10020

This Aladdin edition March 2014

Copyright © 1982 by Frank Asch

For information about special discounts for bulk purchases, please contact

Simon & Schuster Special Sales at 1-866-506-1949 or business@simonandschuster.com.

The Simon & Schuster Speakers Bureau can bring authors to your live event.

For more information or to book an event contact the Simon & Schuster Speakers Bureau

at 1-866-248-3049 or visit our website at www.simonspeakers.com.

Designed by Karina Granda

The text of this book was set in Olympian LT Std.

Manufactured in China 1119 SCP

10 9 8 7 6

Library of Congress Cataloging-in-Publication Data

Asch. Frank.   Happy birthday, moon.

Summary: When a bear discovers the moon shares his birthday,

he buys the moon a beautiful hat as a present.

[1. Bears—Fiction. 2. Moon—Fiction. 3. Birthdays—Fiction.] I. Title

[PZ7.A778Hap 1988] [E] 88-6569

ISBN 978-1-4424-9401-5 (hc)

ISBN 978-1-4424-9400-8 (pbk)

ISBN 978-1-4424-9402-2 (eBook)

To Devin

One night Bear looked up at the sky and thought, *wouldn't it be nice to give the moon a birthday present?*

But Bear didn't know when the moon's birthday was, or what to get him. So he climbed a tall tree to have a little chat with the moon.

"Hello, Moon!" he shouted.

But the moon did not reply.

Maybe I am too far away, thought Bear, *and the moon cannot hear me.*

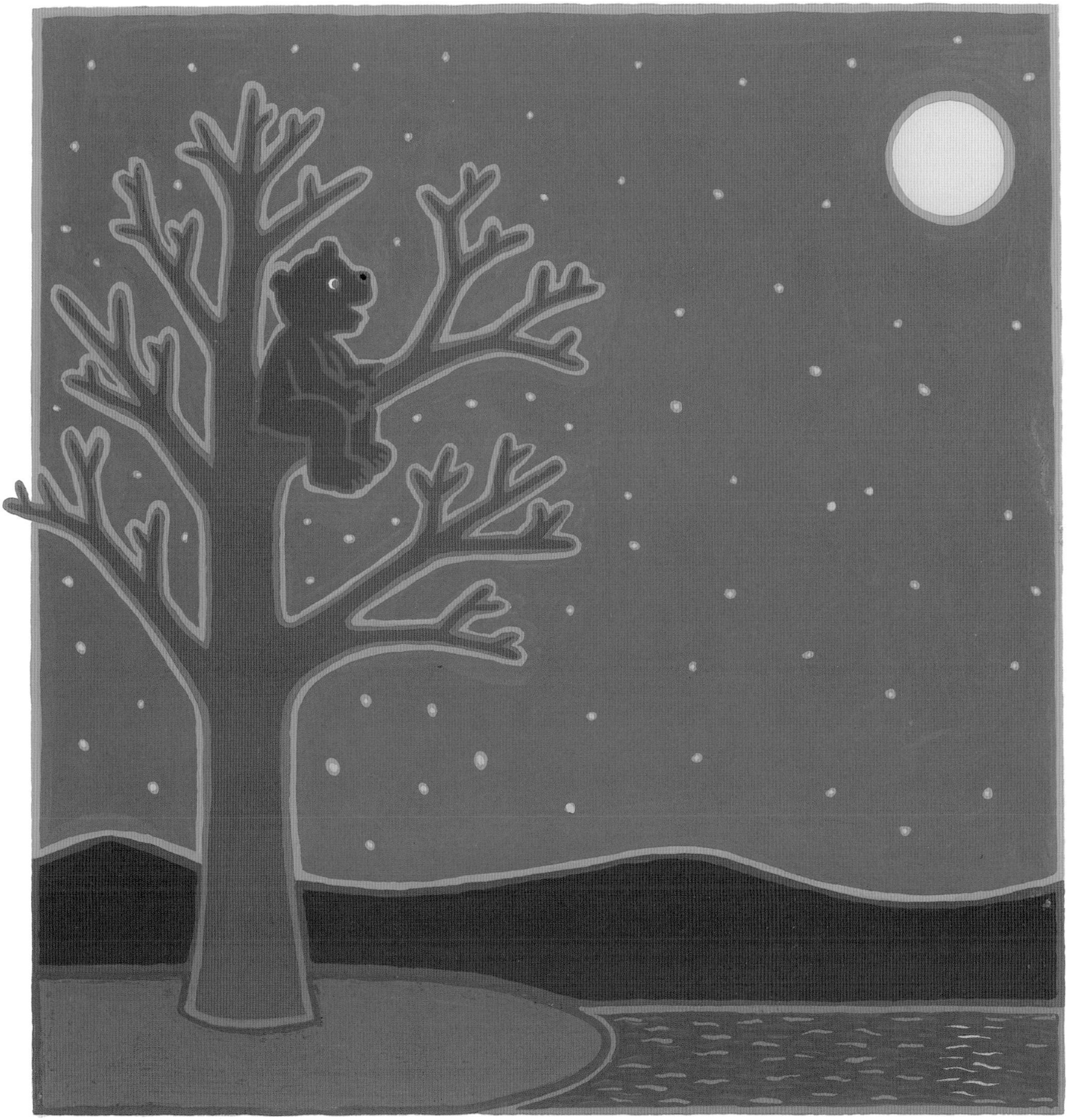

So Bear paddled across the river . . .

and hiked through the forest . . .

into the mountains.

Now I am much closer to the moon, thought Bear, and again he shouted: "Hello!"

This time his own voice echoed off one of the other mountains: "Hello!"

Bear got very excited. *Oh, boy!* he thought, *I'm talking to the moon.*

"Tell me," asked Bear, "when is your birthday?"

"Tell me, when is your birthday?" replied the moon.

"Well, it just so happens that my birthday is tomorrow!" said Bear.

"Well, it just so happens that my birthday is tomorrow!" said the moon.

"What do you want for your birthday?" asked Bear.

"What do you want for your birthday?" asked the moon.

Bear thought for a moment, then he replied: "I would like a hat."

"I would like a hat," said the moon.

Oh, goody! thought Bear, now I know what to get the moon for his birthday.

"Goodbye," said Bear.

"Goodbye," said the moon.

When Bear got home, he dumped all the money out of his piggy bank.

Then he went downtown . . .

and bought the moon a beautiful hat.

That night he put the hat up in a tree where the moon
could find it. Then he waited and watched while the moon

slowly crept up through the branches and tried on the hat.
"Hurray!" yelled Bear. "It fits just right!"

During the night while Bear slept, the hat fell out of the tree.

In the morning Bear found the hat on his doorstep.

"So the moon got me a hat too!" exclaimed Bear.

He tried it on and it fit perfectly.

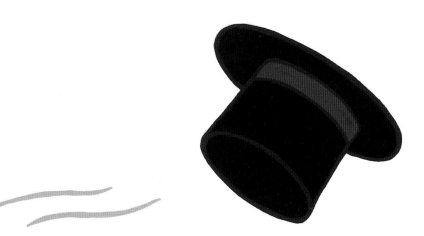

But just then the wind blew Bear's hat off his head.
He chased after it . . .

but it got away.

That night Bear paddled across the river . . .

and hiked through the forest . . .

to talk with the moon.

For a long time the moon would not speak to him, so Bear spoke first. "Hello!" he shouted.

"Hello!" replied the moon.

"I lost the beautiful hat you gave me," said Bear.

"I lost the beautiful hat you gave me," said the moon.

"That's okay, I still love you!" said Bear.

"That's okay, I still love you!" said the moon.